SCHOOL FOR PIRATES

THE SNEAKY SWEET STEALER

CHAE STRATHIE

ILLUSTRATED BY ANNA CHERNYSHOVA

To Cap'n Euan and Cap'n Adam – the finest shipmates a pirate could ask for, and definitely not a pair of slitherin' sea slugs or jabberin' jellyfish!

Scholastic Children's Books
An imprint of Scholastic Ltd
Euston House, 24 Eversholt Street, London, NW1 1DB, UK
Registered office: Westfield Road, Southam, Warwickshire, CV47 0RA
SCHOLASTIC and associated logos are trademarks and/or
registered trademarks of Scholastic Inc.

First published in the UK by Scholastic Ltd, 2017
Text copyright © Chae Strathie, 2017
Interior illustrations copyright © Anna Chernyshova, 2017

Cover illustration copyright © Marta Kissi, 2017

The right of Chae Strathie and Anna Chernyshova to be identified as
the author and illustrator of this work has been asserted by them.

ISBN 978 1407 16340 6

A CIP catalogue record for this book is available from the British Library.

Printed by CPI Group (UK) Ltd, Croydon, CR0 4YY
Papers used by Scholastic Children's Books are made
from wood grown in sustainable forests.

1 3 5 7 9 10 8 6 4 2

This is a work of fiction. Names, characters, places, incidents and
dialogues are products of the author's imagination or are used
fictitiously. Any resemblance to actual people, living or dead,
events or locales is entirely coincidental.

www.scholastic.co.uk

CHAPTER 1

"Where's my parrot?

HAS ANYONE SEEN MY PARROT?"

It was the first day of the new term at Captain Firebeard's School for Pirates and Tommy was late. Again.

"Mum! Have you seen McBeaky?" said Tommy, bursting from his room.

"Well I definitely packed him before we came home yesterday," replied Mum, stopping on her way downstairs. "So we didn't leave him behind at the hotel."

"Packed?" muttered Tommy. "Who packs a parrot?"

Then he stopped.

"Hang on ... I haven't **UN**packed!"

He dashed back into his bedroom, pinged open the catches on his trunk – the one with the skull and cross-bones stickers all over it – and flung open the lid.

"McBeaky!" he yelled.

A yellow sock twitched and squawked softly.

"McBeaky! Is that you?"

"My own ship, you say?"
said the sock.
"McBeaky!"
"Squawk
– call me Cap'n McBeaky."

"MCBEAKY! WAKE UP!"

shouted Tommy, unrolling the sock to reveal a half-asleep parrot.

"Squawk! Thanks a lot. Having a great wee dream I was."

Tommy lifted the ruffled bird out and pointed him towards the poster of Captain Firebeard positioned in pride of place above his bed.

"You know what he'll do to us if we don't get our skates on and make it to

6

the *Rusty Barnacle* before the clock strikes nine?"

McBeaky gulped a small, parroty gulp.

"Plank. Sea. Sharks. Not good," he squawked.

"No. Not good at all," replied Tommy. "So let's go."

He grabbed his bag and his neck scarf and clattered down the stairs to the kitchen.

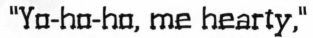

"Yo-ho-ho, me hearty,"
said Dad. "Breakfast is served."

"But there's no time," gasped
Tommy. "I'm going to be late."

"There's Pirate Puffs..." said Dad,
shaking a box temptingly.

"Pirate Puffs? Oh. Ummm. . . Well, I suppose could probably spare a minute or two," said Tommy, sitting down. He **LOVED** Pirate Puffs.

Dad poured the cereal into the bowl while Mum gave McBeaky a plate of chopped banana – his favourite.

Tommy shovelled the Pirate Puffs into his mouth as fast as he could.

"Careful," warned Mum. "You don't want a treasure chest going down the wrong way."

Tommy finished in lightning time and jumped up from the table.

"C'mon McBeaky, let's get a move on," he said.

"MMMFF GllFF bnnAnNNUUFF!"

mumbled the parrot, stuffing banana into his beak as fast as possible.

"Bye, Mum, bye, Dad," said Tommy as he made for the door.

"Bye, love. Watch out for scurvy scoundrels and salty sea dogs," said Mum anxiously.

"And make sure your **"AᴬARRRs"** are nice and clear," added Dad.

Tommy bounded out of the door and ran down the rain-soaked street as McBeaky flew behind him, spraying passers-by with lumps of mashed banana as he went.

The hands on the clock tower were almost at nine. There was no way he was going to make it to school in time.

He was running so fast down the steep hill that he almost crashed into

Mr Sprat the fishmonger.

"Careful, Tommy, lad," chuckled Mr Sprat. "You almost knocked this box of flatfish out of me hands."

A lightbulb suddenly went on over Tommy's head.

"Get your skates on..." he murmured.

A flick of a dolphin's tail later, Tommy was hurtling down the wet cobbles with two large, very slippery fish tied to his shoes with string.

"Beats roller skates!"

he laughed as he bobbed and weaved past alarmed people on the way to the harbour.

As he reached the bottom of the street he spotted the unmistakable wonky shape of the *Rusty Barnacle*, the ship on which Captain Firebeard had his School for Pirates. The other pupils were all on deck and it looked like the anchor was being raised.

BOOOOONNNNGGG!

The clock began to strike nine.

Was he going to make it?

Just as he thought he might get there in time, he saw a figure standing beside the lever that operated the gangplank. A figure that had sharp elbows and a mean pointy chin.

"Spiky Spencer," muttered Tommy as he hunched down like a skier, trying to make himself go even faster.

Spencer gave him a nasty little wave and pushed the lever. The gangplank started to lift and swing back towards the ship.

Oh no, thought Tommy, *I've had it now!*

The ship began to pull away from the dockside. Tommy would never make it.

But then he spotted a plank of wood leaning on a lobster creel.

It looked sort of like a ... ramp.

Tommy hit it at top speed and

shot high into the air. He did a triple somersault, a three-quarter corkscrew, and waved at a gaping-mouthed Spiky Spencer as he sailed over his head upside down.

He landed with a gentle **THUMP** on deck right in front of Captain Firebeard.

BooOOONnNNNGGGGGG!

The clock struck nine.

"Nice of you to join us, Hotshot Tom," growled Captain Firebeard.

"Liking the new shoes," whispered Jo, glancing at his fishy footwear.

Milton gave him a friendly nudge.

"SCHOOL IS IN SESSION,"

shouted Sea Dog Steve. "AAAAARRRRR!"

"AAAAARRRRR!"

bellowed the pupils in unison.
The new term had begun.

CHAPTER 2

Tommy, Jo and Milton clumped downstairs with the rest of the class to the classroom.

"So what did you two get up to during the holidays?" asked Tommy.

"I climbed Mount Terrifying, went diving with sharks and learned to tightrope walk ... over a crocodile-infested river," said Jo.

"Then, after all that relaxing stuff, I went on an adventure holiday with my mum and dad."

Milton looked like he was about to be sick.

He was as nervous as Jo was fearless.

"What about you, Milt?" asked Tommy.

"I, errr, played snap with my gran, but I kept getting a fright when she shouted **'SNAP'**, so we stopped," he said.

"Apart from that I was mainly checking out old pirate maps and learning some new codes and stuff."

"Sure it'll come in handy," smiled Tommy. "In fact, I'll bet—"

But before he could finish his sentence, Spiky Spencer, who had been listening to them from behind, barged through with his sharp elbows.

As usual he was wearing the finest blue velvet uniform, freshly bought for the new term from

SEASPRAY & SMYTHE

OUTFITTERS OF YOUNG GENTLEMAN PIRATES

on Diamond Avenue.

"Huh! My holiday was better than all of your silly holidays put together," he sneered. "I sailed to all the richest and most fabulous islands on my father's enormous yacht. It is the biggest pirate yacht on the Seven Seas and has a vast crew of butlers and maids who fetch whatever you tell them to."

And with that he marched off with

his gang, Muttonhead Max and Greta the Grouch, pushing his way past everyone so he could be first in the classroom.

By the time Tommy, Jo and Milton got there the teachers were waiting for them.

Sea Dog Steve, Captain Firebeard's right-hand (or right-hook) man, was there. So were One-Eyed Norm, the cannon expert, and Magpie Maggie, who was in charge of all things adventurous and had an eye for treasure and sparkling jewels.

The ship's cook, Gumms, was there too, which explained the smell of kippers, cabbage and rotten eggs. Gumms was the worst cook on the Seven Seas ... and on land for that matter.

In front of the teachers stood Captain Firebeard, with his scarlet tunic and **ENORMOUS** orange beard the colour of flame.

"Hurry along, Hotshot Tom, Jo the Fearless and Whizz-kid Milton,"

he grizzled, as Tommy and the others scurried in and slid into their wooden seats at their desks.

Their parrots hopped off their shoulders on to the perches next to them – Tommy's parrot, McBeaky, Jo's parrot, Flash, and Milton's parrot, Wobbles.

"AAAARRRR!"

bellowed Captain Firebeard.

"AAAARRRR!"

replied the class.

"Welcome back to school," he said.

"TIME TO FORGET YER LAND LUBBIN' WAYS AND GET YER SEA LEGS BACK ON."

He stomped his wooden leg on the wooden floor for effect.

STOMP-STOMP!

"Last term you learned plenty o' map readin', cannon-firin' an' pirate history," he continued. "This term you be in line for pirate geography, PE and sea monster classes. And there be a few new teachers you'll meet along the way."

He continued telling the class what to expect that term – and what would be expected of them, including **sensational swashbucklin'** and **brilliant buccaneerin'** – until the ship's bell clanged.

"BREAK-TIME, CLASS."

bellowed Sea Dog Steve. "Off you go."

The pupils jostled out of the classroom and headed straight for the tuck shop.

It was a wooden kiosk at one end of a room above the classrooms and just below the main deck. It was piled high with all sorts of incredible pirate sweets, snacks and juice. It was the pupils' favourite part of the ship.

Of course, Spiky Spencer made sure Muttonhead Max bashed a path to the front of the line for him so he could be first.

"I see nothing's changed since last term," sighed Milton to Jo and Tommy as they waited patiently in the middle of the queue.

"I wish Spiky Spencer had accidentally been eaten by a whale or got a jellyfish in his swimming trunks over the holidays," scowled Jo.

At the tuck-shop kiosk there was a sudden kerfuffle.

"What do you mean there are no Winkleman's Sugar Pearls? I wanted to buy the whole box before anyone else could!" shouted Spiky Spencer.

"Well, tough tuna!" retorted Liquorice Len, who ran the tuck shop. "The box is mysteriously missin' and I 'ave no idea where it be."

"DISGRACEFUL!" whined Spencer.

"It be an even bigger disgrace if it has been **STOLEN,**" snapped Liquorice Len. "The last thing we be wantin' on board the *Rusty Barnacle* is a **SNEAKY SWEET STEALER.**

"ARʀʀʀGɢGʜʜH!"

Tommy, Jo and Milton exchanged glances.

This could be a situation to keep an eye on...

CHAPTER 3

CLANG-A-LANG-A-LANG-A-LANGGGGG!

"Is it really necessary for them to ring the wake-up bell quite so loud?"

groaned Milton from his hammock. "I was having a great dream about solving a complicated series of secret codes."

"Sounds, err ... exciting," yawned Tommy as he swung his legs down.

"Come on you two lazy landlubbers!" shouted Jo as she sprang into the room, giving Milton such a fright that his hammock spun round at high speed before flinging him out into a heap on the floor.

Jo had already been up for an hour practising rigging-climbing and doing triple backflips off the plank.

It was the second week of school and, after several days out at sea, the *Rusty Barnacle* was now anchored in a small, sunny bay with crystal clear water next to **Oyster Island.** Early every morning the Pirate Exercise (PE) teacher, Hurricane Harriet, would lead deck sports – like crow's nest basketball and rigging races – as well as diving and swimming lessons. It was Jo's favourite part of the day.

After a breakfast of rock-hard toast smeared with disgusting mackerel jam made by Gumms, Captain Firebeard called the class on deck.

His enormous orange bristles glowed like a bonfire in the light of the morning sun.

"AAAARRRR!" he bellowed.

"AAAARRRR!" replied the class.

"Excellent AᴬAARᴿRᴿ-ing, me hearties,"

said the captain. "Ye have clearly been practisin' over the holidays.

"Now, we have a special teacher on board this morning. Her name be Crossbones Kate and she knows everythin' there is to know about monsters of the deep.

"She be waitin' to start the lesson down in room three and I want you to listen very carefully."

"Aye, aye, cap'n!"

called the class in unison, before heading below deck to a classroom they'd never been in before.

When the pupils filed into room three, there were large posters of weird and terrifying sea monsters hanging up alongside the usual selection of mysterious maps, charts of long lost islands, lists of secret pirate codes and models of legendary pirate ships.

"Good morning, class," said a small, polite voice. "Please do sit down."

From out of the book cupboard next to the blackboard came a tiny, very neatly dressed pirate lady.

She had tidy grey hair pinned up in a bun and a small round spectacles perched on her nose.

On her shoulder sat a small grey parrot with matching round glasses balanced on its beak.

"My name is Crossbones Kate," said the little teacher, "and we have a lot to fit in, so let's get started straight away."

She pointed with a wooden stick at a detailed drawing of a very, **VERY LARGE** snake-like beast.

"Let's begin nice and easy," she said. "Who can tell me what this is?"

"SEA SERPENT! EASY!"

snapped Spiky Spencer.

Crossbones Kate looked at him over her glasses.

"That is correct," she said. **"However, if you shout out in class without putting your hand up one more time, young man, I shall feed you to my pet Jagsnaggler."**

"Errr, what's a Jagsnaggler?" asked Spencer nervously.

"YOU DON'T WANT TO KNOW," said Crossbones Kate, darkly. "Now, an adult sea serpent can grow up to two hundred feet long and wrap itself around a ship, crushing it as if it was made of ice-lolly sticks. Take notes, everyone. Do keep up."

She pointed her stick at the next picture – an enormous octopus-type monster.

"This is the Giant Squid," she said. "Extremely large and quite annoying, but as long as you steer your ship away from its tentacles, it doesn't usually present a problem."

The next drawing looked sort of similar, but this creature was even bigger and had mean yellow eyes and a huge, gaping mouth with row upon row of long sharp teeth.

"Any thoughts?" asked Crossbones Kate.

Tommy raised his hand.

"Is it a kraken, miss?" he asked.

"Jolly good," said Crossbones Kate. "How did you know?"

"My Auntie Betty gave me a book called **The Pirate's Guide To Horrible Big Beasties That Want To Eat You** for my last birthday," he explained.

"Ahh, know it well," said Crossbones Kate.

"Do you?" asked Tommy.

"Oh yes," said Crossbones Kate. "I wrote it."

Tommy's eyes widened. That was one of his favourite books and here was the person who wrote it, actually teaching him.

Wow!

For the rest of the morning Crossbones Kate told them all about the strange creatures of the deep – from crabs the size of houses to rarer beasts like the mighty ten-headed Whakalaka and the flying Feathered Puffblazer, which could set a ship's sails on fire with one snort from its glowing red snout.

The most mysterious one of all didn't even have a picture.

"They say the Slippery Sneakslider has five hundred long, thin tentacles," explained Crossbones Kate.

"It is huge, but so sneaky and quiet that it has only been glimpsed a handful of times. We're not sure what it eats or even if it is dangerous, but as it's very unlikely that you will ever see one, it's more of a curiosity than anything else."

CLANG!

CLANG!

CLANG!

The ship's bell rang out sharply three times – the sound for the whole class to assemble at once on the main deck.

"Well, we're nearly at the end of the lesson in any case," said Crossbones Kate. "Off you go. Quickly now."

"Wonder what's up?" said Milton as they hurried up the stairs.

"Something tells me it won't be good," said Jo.

"I think you might be right," agreed Tommy as they came out on deck to see Captain Firebeard waiting for them.

He did not look pleased. At. All.

CHAPTER 4

"WE HAVE A THIEF ON BOARD,"

growled Captain Firebeard.

His beard seemed even bigger and fierier than usual, thought Tommy, like a garden hedge that been dipped in orange paint.

A loud **"GULP"** echoed round the deck as everyone swallowed nervously at the same time.

The ship was silent apart from the sound of the light breeze gently flapping the skull-and-crossbones flag that hung from the mast. The sea was perfectly still.

Behind Captain Firebeard, the rest of the teachers stood and looked sternly at the pupils and ship's crew. Nobody dared utter a word.

Captain Firebeard eyed them angrily. "I run a tight ship here and I don't take too kindly to **booty-burgling bilge rats** and **TRICKY TREASURE TAKERS** round these parts," he said. "But we seem to have a scurvy sea slug at work and I mean to find out who it is. And when I do, the fish are going to get a fine feed that day."

Sea Dog Steve saw the confused look on Muttonhead Max's face.

"He means that whoever did it is goin' to walk the plank, Muttonhead," he said.

Everyone jumped as the captain clapped his hands suddenly.

Liquorice Len appeared from a doorway carrying a large wooden case.

Captain Firebeard nodded at him and Len tipped the case upside down.

Nothing fell out.

What on earth was going on?

"Last week this case was full o' sweets and tuck," said Liquorice Len grimly. "But now it be …

EMPTY."

"Somebody has been stealing the sweets," added Sea Dog Steve.

"And that somebody must be aboard this ship," growled Captain Firebeard.

Everyone looked at each other suspiciously.

"Right now we don't know who did it," barked Captain Firebeard. "But mark my words, we will. Now, what exactly is missing, Len?"

Liquorice Len pulled a list out of his pocket.

"Fourteen packets of Crusoe's Coconut Chews, six nets of chocolate doubloons, nine sachets of Cap'n Candy's Gold Dust sherbet, five hundred foam shrimps, an extra-large bag of jelly jellyfish, a jar of sea-salt toffees, a tub of desert island dessert and three bottles of fizzy haddock juice. Oh, and a packet of prawn cocktail crisps."

Whoever was stealing from the tuck shop really had a sweet tooth. Actually, more like a whole mouthful of sweet teeth – if they had any teeth left at all after scoffing that lot!

Captain Firebeard stood with his hands on his hips, tapping his wooden leg angrily.

"That be all for now," he said. "But we be watching you ... and the plank is gettin' tested to make sure it's extra bouncy – perfect for

boinging sweet stealers into sharky
seas. Class and crew dismissed.

"AᴬAARʀRʀ!"

"AAAARRR,"

came the nervous response.

Tommy, Jo and Milton gathered
together.

"Who do you think did it?" asked
Milton.

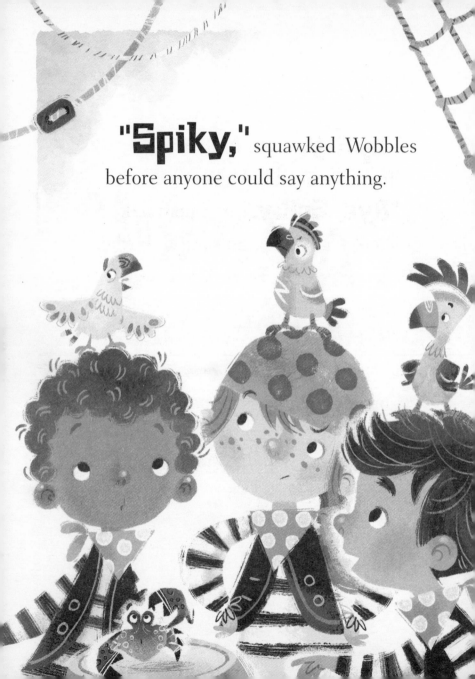

"Spiky," squawked Wobbles before anyone could say anything.

"Spiky," squawked Flash.

Tommy looked at McBeaky.

"Aye, Spiky," he squawked.

"Looks like the parrots are sure who did it – even if the teachers aren't," said Jo.

"Well what are we going to do about it?" said Tommy. "We can't have someone stealing all the jelly jellyfish – they're my favourite. Mind you, he's welcome to the fizzy haddock juice –

BLEURRRGH!"

"We'll just have to keep an eye on him," said Jo. "See if we can spot him acting suspiciously."

"He won't get away with it," said Milton.

"The sneaky sweet stealer will be caught!" said Tommy. "Spikey Spencer, your plundering days are numbered!"

CHAPTER 5

- Jolly Roger's Fizzy Fish Gums
- Everlasting cannonball gobstoppers
- Buccaneer Bubblegum
- Super-sour chewy pieces of eight
- Hornpipe and Co.'s Famous White Chocolate Anchors

The list of sweets that were stolen got longer and longer as the term went on. But still no one was caught.

Captain Firebeard and the other teachers checked lockers and pockets, hammocks, school bags and even the crow's nest – but they never found any clues.

No wrappers, no half-chewed chews, no telltale smears of stickiness or trails of sugar.

Every day Captain Firebeard's beard seemed to bristle bigger and bigger and glow as crimson as a South Seas sunset.

One morning the pupils headed below for their pirate geography lesson. Magpie Maggie was waiting for them in the classroom. She'd placed a large, leather-bound book on every desk.

"AHOY, SHIPMATES," she said. "Hurry up, you slow sea snails, come on, sit down, sit down. Turn to page twelve and let's set sail on a voyage to a very special place."

Everyone flipped through the old yellow pages of the books. They were filled with beautiful maps, complicated charts and pictures of incredible-looking islands and ports.

On page twelve there was a drawing of a hotchpotch of houses of all shapes and size crammed together with twisting dark alleys between them and all sorts of pirates bustling around. On the opposite page was a detailed map of a town's streets.

"This be the pirate capital – **Plunderossa,** on the island of Scaratoga," said Magpie Maggie. "It be an **INCREDIBLE** place, full o' fun and laughter, where the windin' streets echo to the sound o' sea shanties day and night and there be so much **TREASURE** the door knobs are made o' rubies and—"

"My father says it's full of scallywags and ruffians," snapped Spiky Spencer. He had just come into the classroom after being laid up in bed with a sore tummy that morning (Gumms had created a particularly smelly blue-cheese and squid pie the night before, so everyone felt a bit queasy).

Plunderossa

-13-

"Aye, that it be," said Magpie Maggie. Then she laughed. "Which is why it be my favourite place on earth! "AᴬAARʀRʀ!"

As the lesson went on, Maggie told them all about Plunderossa.

Tommy wrote everything down in his jotter.

"The Mayor of Plunderossa is Jake Sharkbeard, who was a great pirate before he became Mayor.

"The town is famous for its enormous Plunderossa Pizzas – each one is big enough to feed a whole crew.

"The liveliest area is **YOHO** and the most mysterious area is **Silvermoon Lane**, which some people say is full of **MAGIC**.

"Plunderossa Museum is full of **AMAZING** things, like a full-size moving model of a kraken and a very unusual clockwork galleon made by the great inventor Captain Spannerbeard..."

The pupils jumped in fright as Captain Firebeard crashed through the classroom door.

He stomp-clomped to the front of the class, his wooden leg bashing the floorboards. He spun round and faced the pupils with a dark scowl on his red-bearded face. There was a soft **"Plomp"**

as Milton's parrot, Wobbles, who was a nervous as Milton was, fainted and fell off his owner's shoulder on to the desk.

"There has been another theft from the tuck shop," Firebeard growled. "A whole box o' Gold Nugget Poppin' Candy."

He started walking slowly down the space between the desks.

THUMP, CLOMP. THUMP, CLOMP.
THUMP, CLOMP.

"But this time we has found the culprit!"

A **GASP** went round the room.

"The sneaky sweet stealer has slipped up this time and not got rid o' the clues."

THUMP, CLOMP.

THUMP, CLOMP.

"When I found out whose locker the poppin' candy was in I must admit my timbers was so shivered they almost turned to sawdust. But evidence be evidence..."

THUMP, CLOMP.

"And the name of the thief is..."

CLOMP.

Captain Firebeard stopped. He lifted his hand and pointed a large hairy finger.

"What?" exclaimed Tommy. **"No! B-b-but I... It wasn't..."**

"There's been a mistake!"

shouted Jo.

"Tommy wouldn't do that!"

gasped Milton.

"I told you he was a rotten apple," sniggered Spiky Spencer.

Captain Firebeard clapped his hands and two burly pirates came into the room.

"Take him to the Naughty Pirate's Room in the hold and keep an eye on him," he said.

At the mention of the Naughty Pirate's Room the class let out gasp. Nobody wanted to end up down in the hold. It was chilly and smelled of a haddock's underpants. If haddock wore underpants.

Captain Firebeard looked down at Tommy as he was led away. "I'm disappointed in ye, lad. I really thought you could make a magnificent pirate one day."

Tommy gulped. It looked like his time on the *Rusty Barnacle* was almost at an end.

CHAPTER 6

"CRABSTICKS AND FISH HEADS!"

"OCTOPUS TENTACLES AND SCURVY WHELKS!"

"BILGE RATS AND SMELLY SEAWEED!"

"SQUID POOP AND HERRINGS' BUMS!"

"Do herring have bums?"
"I don't know. It doesn't matter, Milton." Jo sighed.

They were sitting in a little
tree-house type of hut halfway up
the small mast at the back of the
ship, letting out their anger at what
had happened to Tommy.

Jo had wanted to go up to the crow's nest on the main mast, but there was no **WAY** Milton, or Wobbles, would go anywhere that high up. Even the small mast was enough to give him the knee-jiggles.

The sun was just starting to sink beneath the horizon and the sky was turning as orange as you-know-who's whiskers. Tomorrow the *Rusty Barnacle* would set sail for home – back to Piratehaven – where Tommy would be put ashore and never be allowed to set foot on board again.

No matter how much Jo and Milton had pleaded with the teachers, they insisted that the evidence was there, clear as day. Tommy was the one who had been stealing the sweets from the tuck shop.

"This stinks more than Gumms's pickled egg and raw onion trifle," said Jo.

But Milton wasn't listening.

"Shhhh!" he said. "Can you hear that?"

Jo listened. There were hushed voices from the bottom of the mast. It was Spiky Spencer – she'd recognize that voice anywhere.

"I can't hear what they're saying, but it sounds like they're up to something, whatever it is," she said.

Milton looked around the mast-hut.

"I have an idea," he said. He picked up a long length of hose that was coiled in the corner.

"The great thing about hoses is you can use them for cleaning things ... or for listening in on conversations," he said. "Pass me that funnel."

Jo picked up a bashed copper funnel and tossed it to Milton, who wedged it into one end of the hosepipe.

Then he ever so gently slid it out of the open window and fed it through his hands.

"STOP!" whispered Jo, who was

peering down at Spiky Spencer, Greta
the Grouch and Muttonhead Max.
"It's there."

Milton held the end of the pipe to his ear.

"I can hear them perfectly!" he yelped.

"What are they saying?" urged Jo.

Milton listened.

"Hang on ... they think it's really funny that Tommy is in the Naughty Pirates' Room ... can't wait to see the back of him ... little pipsqueak ... their plan worked perfectly..."

"PLAN? WHAT PLAN?" hissed Jo.

"Shhh! Spencer's saying he loved

the look on Tommy's face when old Firebeard pointed at him ... nobody even guessed that **HE'D** stolen the popping candy and hidden it in Tommy's locker so he'd get in trouble. Why the horrible... We have to tell one of the teachers."

Jo thought for a moment. "They won't believe us," she said. "We have no proof."

"Wait a minute," whispered Milton. "They're saying they're going back to the tuck shop tonight to steal more sweets and put them in **OUR** lockers so we get put ashore too!"

JO'S GREEN EYES FLASHED.

"Not if we catch them in the act," she said calmly. "But first let's get Tommy out of that room."

As soon as Spencer and his gang had gone, Jo and Milton swung down the rigging – or at least Jo did. Milton edged down incredibly slowly, with his eyes shut.

Dusk settled softly over the ship and the oil lamps were lit in the windows of the teachers' quarters. Jo whistled quietly – low, high and low again.

There was a flap of wings in the dim light and McBeaky, Flash and Wobbles appeared.

Jo spoke quickly. "We need to set Tommy free so he can help us catch Spiky Spencer and his gang stealing more sweets," she said. "It was Spencer who put the popping candy in Tommy's locker."

"Told you!" the three parrots squawked in unison.

"We need you to get down to the

hold," continued Jo. "Then find the big bunch of keys and carry them over to the Naughty Pirates' Room. It will take two of you – the other should be on lookout, just in case. Drop the keys through the hatch on the door and tell Tommy to meet us behind the wooden crates opposite the tuck shop."

"Aye, aye, Jo the Fearless!" squawked McBeaky.

"PARROTS, HO!"

At that, the three fluttered off down the hatch towards the hold.

"Do you think it'll work?" asked Milton doubtfully.

"We'll soon find out," said Jo.

Milton bunched his fist and held it out in front of him towards Jo.

"Pirates for ever," he said.

Jo pressed her knuckles against his in the traditional pirate handshake.

"Pirates for ever," she repeated.

"LET'S GO!"

It was time to catch a sneak.

{ CHAPTER 7 }

CReAK...
CReeeAAAK...
CREAK-
A-CReEE
EEAAAAAAK!

The boat was rolling gently back and forth on the evening tide and the old twisted wood of the decks and hull croaked and creaked. It was the only sound to be heard in the otherwise silent canteen, outside the galley.

Jo and Milton were hiding behind a stack of empty sweet crates opposite the tuck shop. Shafts of silver moonlight shone through the portholes lighting up shelves stacked with goodies.

"Just one," whispered Jo, gazing at a pile of marshmallow treasure chests.

"I really don't think we should help ourselves to the sweets," said Milton quietly. "That would make us just as bad as the thieves."

"I know," sighed Jo. "I wish they didn't look so yummy though."

"Please stop thinking about sweets and concentrate," hissed Milton. "We need to listen for Spiky Spencer and the others. Let's go through the plan one more time."

"Yes, yes," said Jo. "When they have the sweets in their hands you pull the string attached to the bell and all the teachers will come running. We've been over this **SEVENTEEN** times."

"HAVE NOT!" said Milton. "It's only been **sixteen** times."

He shuffled his bottom, trying to get comfortable.

"Where are those parrots?" he said. "Do you think they've been caught?"

"I think we'd have heard about it by now," said Jo. "Wobbles probably just got frightened by a bit of fluff or something and dropped the keys."

Milton was about to say something about not being rude about Wobbles when there was a sound from the far end of the room. **"Shhh,"** hissed Jo.

"Keep your eyes peeled. And get ready with that string."

The door in the far corner – the one that led down to the sleeping quarters – opened a crack.

From their hiding place behind the crates Jo and Milton could see an eye appear at the crack. Then another below it. And another above it.

The door nudged open a little more and the three eyes became three heads cautiously poking into the gap.

Spiky Spencer in the middle, Greta the Grouch below him and Muttonhead Max above.

Milton let out a **squeak.**

"Shhh!" Jo whispered. "Here they come."

The three sneaky sneaks sneaked into the room one by one.

Greta stayed by the door, keeping an eye out in case any of the teachers appeared, while Spencer and Max crept over to the tuck shop.

"What shall we take?" said Max.

"Hmmm, I think Milton should have marshmallows – he's probably scared of fizzy sweets. And for Josephine some **super-sour barnacle gums.**"

Jo scowled. Milton held a finger to his lips and shook his head.

Spencer and Max reached for the sweets and Jo nodded to Milton. Milton lifted the string slowly and...

A hand landed on his shoulder.

"YEEEEEE EEAAAAAA AHOOO HAAAA!"

he screeched, leaping at least four feet in the air.

"Quiet," said Tommy. **"It's only me."**

"It's a bit late for being quiet," said Spiky Spencer, striding across the room with Muttonhead Max and Greta behind him.

"Sorry we're late," squawked McBeaky, flapping into the room.

"Wobbles got frightened by a bit of fluff and dropped the ... oh."

"Spy on us, would you," said Spencer. "You little whelks are for it. How would you like a dunk in a barrel of Gumms's used fish oil?"

Max cracked his huge knuckles and walked forward.

Just at that moment there was a sound behind them.

Had Captain Firebeard heard all the noise?

Everyone stared at the other end of the room, but there was no one there. There was another **MUFFLED** sound **–A SLIPPERY, SLITHERY THUD –** and one of the portholes beside the tuck shop swung open. A long, wet, green tentacle slid in and twisted its way to a large bag of chocolate beach pebbles.

It curled round the bag, and in one swift movement the tentacle and sweets disappeared out of the window.

The six pupils and three parrots watched with wide eyes and even wider mouths.

"Is everyone seeing what I'm seeing?" said Milton.

"It can't be..." said Tommy. "I think this must be a weird dream caused by something rotten Gumms fed us."

Even as he said this, another porthole opened. Then another ... and another.

A tentacle appeared through each one. Then a lot more slithered down the short staircase from the deck. Then a whole bunch twisted in through a square hatch in the ceiling.

There were tentacles everywhere ... and they were all heading for the sweets.

"You know what you should do, Milton?" said Jo.

"What?" said Milton, staring at the twirling tentacles as if in a trance.

"RING THE BELL!"

Milton snapped out of it, grabbed the string and pulled for all he was worth.

CLANG-A -CLANG- A-CLANG!

{ CHAPTER 8 }

The sound of heavy footsteps crashed up the stairs.

WHAM!

The door flew open and Captain Firebeard strode into the room followed by all the teachers, pupils and crew.

He was about to bellow something loud and probably very angry and fiery, not to mention beardy, when he saw dozens of tentacles squirming around the room.

"Oh," he said. "That I did not expect."

At the sound of the bell, and the din of the teachers barging in, the tentacles had started to slip and slither away. But they clearly weren't keen on letting go of their stolen booty.

Tubs and jars, boxes, bags and bars – they were all being hauled away by whatever greedy creature the tentacles belonged to.

Liquorice Len wasn't about to give up without a fight, though.

As a big tub of candy ruby rings slithered past, he leapt forward and grabbed hold of them.

"GIVE ME THEM BACK, YOU SLIPPERY GREEN BLAGGARD YOU!"

he cried.

But the tentacle didn't want to give them back and it hauled even harder.

141

Len dug his heels in and dragged
the box a few feet back into
to the room.

But the tentacle wasn't listening – and neither was the beastie it was attached to.

Before anyone could do anything, the tentacle gave an almighty tug and the box of sweets, with Len still clinging to it, disappeared up the stairs and away.

The other tentacles quickly followed, popping out of portholes and slithering up through the hatch in the ceiling.

"QUICK,"

bellowed Captain Firebeard.
"ALL PIRATES ON DECK!"
Everyone piled out of the door and up the stairs.

Well, almost everyone. Spiky Spencer, Greta and Max quietly sneaked away.

Outside an enormous full moon lit up the sea and the deck almost as if it was daytime.

The teachers, pupils and crew

spilled out of the door just in time to
see Liquorice Len sliding along the
deck at high speed, still clutching his
sweets.

"Let go, Len!"

shouted Magpie Maggie.

"We'll get you some more candy rings!"

hollered Sea Dog Steve.

But Len wouldn't give up.

He disappeared over the side of the ship in the blink of an eel's eye.

A moment later there was a loud

SPLASH,

"ALL HANDS TO THE STARBOARD SIDE!"

barked Captain Firebeard.

Everyone dashed over to the

handrail. The *Rusty Barnacle* creaked and tilted slightly.

At first there was silence. The sea was still. Len and the creature were nowhere to be seen.

Suddenly, in a froth of water and foam, Len appeared, still clutching his box of sweets.

cheered a small girl next to Tommy.

The tentacle, which was also still clutching the box, lifted Len high out of the water and gave him and the sweets a jiggle.

"NOT YAY," said the same small girl.

Another tentacle curled up and wrapped itself around Len's legs, turning him and the box of sweets upside down. A shower of gleaming red candy ruby rings tumbled into the water. The sea began to bubble. Then an enormous round mouth appeared, followed by an even more enormous green head.

Three huge oval yellow eyes gazed greedily at the candy rings floating on the surface of the sea, before with a great

"SHHHLLL LUUURRRP!"

the mouth hoovered them all up.

"Somebody do something!" cried Squeezebox Serge, the music teacher.

But nobody knew what to do.

The creature was enormous. And it seemed to have hundreds and hundreds of tentacles.

"I ain't never seen so many tentacles on a beastie – and I ain't never seen a beastie like that," said One-Eyed Norm in awe.

"Hang on," said Tommy. "Hundreds of tentacles. Very sneaky and slithery. No one knows what it is...

IT'S A SLIPPERY SNEAKSLIDER!"

"Goodness gracious, I think you're right!" said Crossbones Kate. "Now I can add its picture to my book."

"That's great," said Jo. "But we still need to help Liquorice Len."

Everyone looked at Milton.

Milton scratched his head.

Then he scratched his chin.

Last of all he scratched his nose.

That seemed to help.

"I'VE GOT IT!"

he declared, holding a finger up.

"**GET A CANNON READY!**"

"**WHOA THERE!**" exclaimed Jo. "We can't do that."

"Don't worry," said Milton. "I think I know what's been going on, and how we can save Len. I need as many custard doughnuts as we can get – and Hotshot Tom, I need your help."

"Just tell me what I can do," said Tommy with a gleam in his eye.

The rescue mission was on!

CHAPTER 9

"CUSTARD DOUGHNUT COMIN' THROUGH, AAAARRRR!"

The cry went up as another sugary ball – the kind the class used instead of cannonballs in target practice in their first term – was passed along a chain of pirates from the hold to the deck.

Already there was a pile as high as a whale's eye next to the cannon that had been dragged across to point towards the Slippery Sneakslider.

Poor Len was being juggled through the air from one tentacle to the next as the massive creature slurped on the candy rings.

"I've got an 'orrible feelin' that once the beastie's finished nibblin' those sweets it'll start nibblin' old Len," said Sea Dog Steve.

"Not if we can help it," said Milton.

"What's yer plan, lad?"

asked Captain Firebeard.

"Well," began Milton. "I don't think our terrifying sea monster is quite as scary as it seems. It looks to me like it's the one that has been stealing all those goodies, which makes me think it must have a sweet tooth. Perhaps it just needs to really get a proper fill of sweet stuff to satisfy it."

"Interestin'," said Captain Firebeard. "Let's give it a bash."

Milton looked at Tommy. "You're the best shot on this ship, Tommy. We need to get as many of those doughnuts in the monster's mouth as we can before he even thinks about tasting Len to see if he really is made of liquorice!"

Tommy didn't need asking twice.

"Aye, aye, Whizz-kid Milt,"

he exclaimed, before shouting,

"LOAD THE CANNON!"

Two pirates rolled a fat doughnut into the mouth of the gun while another lit the fuse.

"Doughnut in the hole!"

the pirate shouted.

Tommy took careful aim. He swung the cannon left a bit ... then up a little ... then ...

BANG!

The cannon fired and the doughnut
flew through the air.

SPLASH.

It hit the water just behind the
monster and sank with a loud glug.

"Rats!" said Tommy.
"HEEELLLLP!" wailed
Liquorice Len as the monster

swallowed the last of the candy rings in one go.

"Keep calm, laddie," shouted Captain Firebeard.

Tommy waited until another doughnut was loaded.

He took a deep breath, then swivelled the cannon until he got it just right, then ...

BANG!

The doughnut curved across the night sky and – SPLAT! – it hit Len!

The sea monster licked its lips and lowered the custard-covered pirate towards its gaping mouth.

"I'M DONE FOR!"

Len cried.

Jo placed a hand on Tommy's shoulder. "I know you can do it Tommy," she whispered. "You're the best there is."

Tommy narrowed his eyes as another doughnut was loaded.

Then he closed them altogether. He was going to use his pirate sense.

"Get ready to say ahoy to a doughnut, monster," he said as he listened for the sound of the monster splashing and slurping being carried on the breeze.

BANG!

Everyone held their breath as the doughnut spiralled over the waves.

GULP!

It landed slap-bang in the middle of the monster's mouth – just as Liquorice Len's legs were dangling above it. The monster chewed the doughnut, then swallowed it down.

"MMMM MMM!"

A contented noise rumbled forth from the sea creature as its yellow eyes widened in pleased surprise.

"It likes it!" said Tommy.

"Quick – I need more doughnuts!"

The pirates shovelled more in and Tommy blasted them again and again at the monster.

Before long its cheeks were bulging with sticky custard and sweet dough.

Still Tommy kept firing, and as one doughnut flew high over its head the creature made a grab for it with a tentacle – the tentacle holding Len!

The terrified pirate dropped into the sea as the beast caught it's new custardy prize.

"Oh no!"

cried Magpie Maggie. "Len can't swim!"

"WHAT? A PIRATE WHAT CAN'T SWIM?"

gasped the PE teacher, Hurricane Harriet. "Guess who'll be getting lessons first thing tomorrow morning?"

"Allow me," said Jo, stepping forward.

She did a triple back somersault off the side of the ship and plunged into the water like a dolphin.

As Jo got on with saving Len the monster was already starting to calm down. A contented smile spread across its big green face.

"I think it's had its fill," said Milton with a relieved sigh.

The monster glided over to the side of the ship and bobbed up out of the water until it was almost at the height of the deck.

It gazed lovingly at Tommy, who leaned over and stroked its nose.

"GRRRRRR-GRRRRRRRRRRR!"

the creature softly burbled.

"What's that sound?" asked Sea Dog Steve.

"I think it be purring!"

laughed Captain Firebeard.

"Well I never!"

There was a splish-splash from below.

"Excuse me,"

called Jo's voice. "Can we have a little, you know, help and stuff? Maybe? If it's not too much bother."

The monster looked down. Then a moment later Jo and Liquorice Len appeared, cradled gently in a tentacle.

"This has been quite a night," said Captain Firebeard. "I think we all needs to get to bed and have a good night's sleep."

He strode towards the door to the sleeping quarters where he stopped and turned. "And then I think there's a lot of explainin' to be done."

He was about to leave when a shout came up from across the deck.

It was Gumms.

"Look what that sea beastie found hiding in me barrels of extra-stinky fish oil," he said.

Spiky Spencer, Muttonhead Max and Greta the Grouch were

wriggling away furiously with a tentacle wrapped around each of their waists. They were covered in fishy

ooze and looked very, very unhappy
indeed.

Captain Firebeard's orange whiskers

bristled and bulged. "I'll be havin'
a word with you three," he
growled. "After you have a
VERY good scrubbing down,
that is."

And with that he turned and
stomped below deck.

CHAPTER 10

The *Rusty Barnacle* sailed into Piratehaven to cheers and whoops from the parents who lined the harbour wall.

Another term was at an end.

Tommy, Jo and Milton stood together on deck, leaning over the rail. They waved as they saw their

185

families waiting for them to dock.

"Well, that was an unusual end to the term," said Jo. "Who'd have thought we'd end up with a pet sea monster?"

"Who'd have thought that it wasn't Spiky Spencer stealing the sweets all along?" said Milton.

"Ah, but it was him who stole the popping candy to get me in trouble, so he's not exactly squeaky clean," Tommy pointed out.

Jo smiled, "At least Captain

Firebeard believed us in the end."

"Yep," laughed Tommy. "Turns out it's quite hard to explain why you're hiding in barrels of fish oil."

There was a gentle **THUD** as the boat bumped against the harbour wall. Ropes were thrown ashore and tied up with great pirate knots. The gangplank swung out and rested on the dockside.

Parents and other family members thronged on board, hugging their little pirates and clucking and fussing over them, straightening neckerchiefs and wiping smears of custard from their waistcoats.

A hush fell over the crowd as Captain Firebeard appeared on the upper deck next to the ship's wheel.

"AAAAARRRRR!"

he bellowed.

"AAA AARR RRR!"

called his pupils. The parents beamed proudly.

"It's the end of another term and it's been a lively one and no mistake," he said. "As usual we have certificates for them pupils that has done perfect pirating, which the teachers are handin' out as I speak."

After the **BUCCANEER BRILLIANCE LEVEL TWO** certificates had been given to everyone, the captain climbed down the stairs to the main deck.

"Now it be my pleasure to once again present three special awards for **OUTSTANDING PIRATING**, above and beyond the Pirates' Code."

He walked along the line of pupils.

"I have three *Silver Earring Awards* to give today – one for quick thinking in a time of danger, one for bravery to save a soul at sea, and one for sharp shooting of a cannon under extreme pressure."

He stopped and turned towards the three friends. "Whizz-kid Milton, Jo the Fearless and Hotshot Tom, I am honoured to present you with these special awards."

He handed a silver hoop to each of them.

Then he put a hand on Tommy's

shoulder and leaned in. In a low voice he said, "And I'm sorry I ever doubted you, lad. You're a fine pirate and I shan't make the same mistake twice."

As a rousing round of applause and more cheers went up from the families, Tommy, Jo and Milton slipped away to a quiet spot behind a coil of rope.

"Phew! I can't believe that's another term over already," said Milton.

"I know!" said Jo. "Maybe next term will be nice and quiet."

They all looked at each other and shook their heads.

"Nah!" they all said at the same time.

Jo looked around. "By the way," she said. "Where are Spencer and the other two?"

Tommy put his fingers in his mouth and whistled sharply. From the hatch that led down to the ship's hold three tentacles rose up.

Dangling from the end of one was Spiky Spencer, with Muttonhead Max and Greta the Grouch on the others.

"Just wait until my father hears about this!" screeched Spencer.

"He'll buy this whole ship and have it turned into firewood!"

"Well I hope he has something that will wash away the smell of fish oil before you speak to him," said Tommy.

He whistled again and the tentacles took Spencer and his cronies off to Gumms's galley to carry out their punishment – scrubbing the sticky sea-snail porridge and crusty kipper stew leftovers from dozens of the grubby cook's oldest and most disgusting pots and pans.

They were lucky that Captain Firebeard had decided to not put them off the boat for good.

The ship's bell rang.

CLANG-A-LANG -A-LANG!

"Time to go," said Milton.

Jo put her fist out. "Pirates for ever," she said.

Tommy and Milton put their fists out so they were all touching.

"Pirates for ever," they said together. **"And parrots for ever!"** squawked their parrots.

And with that they headed down
the gangplank and back on to dry land
... until next term.

THE END

Cap'n Chae Strathie regularly sails the
Seven Seas in his trusty ship, the *Inky
Nib*, shouting "ARRRRRR!" at passing
seagulls and writing stories about the
pirates he meets on his adventures.
He has a black-belt in swashbuckling
and timber-shivering and has a parrot
called Scribbles. When he is ashore
he lives in a village in Fife, Scotland,
with a bunch o' landlubbers and some
cats. Arrrrrr!

Cap'n Anna Chernyshova is a sea artist through and through. You'll find her in the crow's nest, drawing everything she spies – from slippery sea monsters to blistering barnacles. When she's not adventuring the globe and sketching portraits of famous pirates, she's moored in Cambridge with her family and salty sea dog McStinky.